For Cesare

Chicago Syndicate, Volume 0.5

Soraya Naomi

Published by Soraya Naomi, 2017.

"True love always makes a man better, no matter what woman inspires it." ~ Alexandre Dumas.

CHAPTER 1

Cesare – present day

I MAKE MY WAY THROUGH the crowd in this palatial white mansion on the outskirts of East Hampton Village to greet my boss in the back of the sunken living room. The entire crew is here, including all the high-ranking members of the New York Syndicate: Michael, the boss; me, the underboss; Luciano, the counselor; and the captains.

Everyone's in attendance with either his spouse or a date for the announcement of Michael's wedding. My date is trailing behind me.

"Michael," I greet him, standing near the fireplace, and stop next to him.

"We're waiting for Joey," Michael says, buttoning up his expensive, tailored suit, with his slender, blonde fiancée, Rachel, standing beside him.

Suddenly, a prickling awareness raises the hairs on the back of my neck, and I turn my head to Joey as he approaches us.

Behind him is his companion, and my blood turns ice-cold when I recognize the beauty in a skin tight blue dress with black hair just as dark as mine and ashy-grey eyes.

What the fuck is Kinsey doing here?

She's the last person I ever expected to see again. And she's also the one person who's never escaped my memory. But as underboss of the New York Syndicate, I must retain my composure.

She's looking around and smiling, and then her eyes widen as they land on me.

I cock my head to her, and she freezes.

It's been five long years since I've seen her, and her presence affects me still. Time is suspended while emotions rage inside me. I grit my teeth, going to Joey and her. Holding my self-control is impossible as I'm reunited with my best and oldest friend. The girl I've known since I was twelve. The woman I've cursed as much as I've loved her.

Kinsey steps behind Joey while he's in conversation with another man, and I grab her arm, towering over her with my six feet of height. "What the hell are you doing here?"

She tries to break free but sways on her legs and slurs, "Get your hands off me!"

Is she drunk?

After releasing her arm, I hiss, "You don't belong here—"

My rant is interrupted by a loud bang. Then shots ring out, and mayhem ensues. Ducking down, I snatch my Smith & Wesson from the back waistband of my pants where it's hidden underneath my suit jacket. And I pull Kinsey down with me, shielding her with my body while pushing her to hide behind the white leather sofa. People scream and dodge behind furniture while uninvited men barge inside Michael's house, smoke and glass bursting around us as they recklessly spray the room with gunfire. Kinsey is hunched down beneath me, vibrating in shock, as I cock my gun, peek over the couch, and fire. But shooting is proving to be difficult with our own people running around.

"Cesare?!" I hear a man calling me.

I turn my head to the hall, and one of our soldiers slides an automatic weapon across the floor. Hurriedly, I snatch it up and fire a round.

He then gives our other members new weapons, and bullets fly free while everything around us is in chaos. Smoke drifts before my eyes, and I keep covering Kinsey.

Abruptly, I hear a loud roar and crane my neck to see Michael, kneeling and pressing his hand on his fiancée's chest that's covered in blood while my captains kill two men.

"You stay here!" I order Kinsey.

She lifts her head and nods unsteadily.

Inching around the couch, I shoot two more attackers while spotting many dead bodies.

"Stop! We've got them!" One of my captains shouts as the last shot rings out.

Keeping my gun aimed, I rise while checking left and right. Blood covers the windows and floor tiles. Other members continue to target their weapons as we peruse the room.

"Go check the other areas of the house," I order four captains.

Then I hurry to Michael, who's sitting quietly on the floor with a dead Rachel in his lap.

My gaze flies to the couch where Joey is now with Kinsey. Focusing is proving to be difficult when I want to smash him for touching her face. But I have more important matters at hand.

"Michael..." I crouch down, just as he explodes, his features set in a hard line.

"What the fuck happened?! Who were they? Lock this fucking place right now. No one leaves!" He rises and lifts Rachel onto the couch. "Look what they did! Are any of the attackers alive? I want one alive. Everyone to the living room!"

I close the distance between us and touch his shoulder. "I'm sorry, Michael, but you need to get a hold of yourself. *Dobbiamo mantenere la calma.*" We need to stay calm.

Michael takes a deep breath, and I can see him struggling. We are the boss and underboss and must always remain in control in front of our men.

"How the hell did they get in? Get past my security? We must have a spy. Who's new here? If you brought someone besides your spouse, line them up against the back wall for questioning," Michael commands.

Following Michael's orders, all of our unmarried members line up their dates, but as I inspect the carnage for mine, I see her dead on the floor.

Meanwhile, Michael scrutinizes each face and, one by one, asks questions to trembling women. The fifth woman is Kinsey.

"You walked in just before we were attacked. Who are you?" Michael demands.

Kinsey's the only one that answers with bite, "Kinsey. I came with Joey." And she looks at him, then at me.

"How do you know her, Joey?"

"She's a friend."

Kinsey and I stare at one another because I'm simply unable to look away.

"Do you two know each other?" Michael asks, his gaze landing on me.

"Yes," I answer as I'm bombarded with fifteen years' worth of memories.

I've known her since I was twelve. I know her better than she knows herself.

CHAPTER 2

Cesare – 15 years ago – age 12

"SHE'S PRETTY!" TONY says, strolling beside me down the hall after class.

We pass the blonde girl in question, who smiles sweetly at me. And I elbow Tony while he gawks at her, so he playfully shoves me to the side.

"Watch it!"

I barrel into a girl who's standing in front of her locker.

"Sorry." I step back hurriedly. Because she's so small, I'm afraid I've crushed her.

She scowls at me, then continues putting her books into her backpack.

I turn and move to catch up with Tony, who's reached the front entrance of the school, when I overhear her mutter, "Asshole."

So I spin back around. "I *said* I was sorry."

She gives me a sidelong glance. "Fine, Cesare."

For a second, I'm amazed. This girl, whose name I don't even know, is the first person that's ever pronounced my name right. *Tjezaray*, not *Ceezar*.

"Hey, you got my name right!"

"Well, yes, I *do* know my history."

"What?" I have no idea what she's talking about, and apparently, that's written all over my face.

"Cesare Borgia? Don't you know the origin of your name?" she asks as if I'm the dumbest boy in school.

"Um... No."

"Cesare Borgia was the illegitimate son of Pope Alexander VI and supposedly had an affair with his own sister." She slams the locker door closed and walks off.

"Really?" Wow, I never expected her to say that, and I decide to go after her. "What's your name?"

"Kinsey," she replies while pushing through the door and hurrying away.

Outside, instead of catching up with Tony, I continue to trail her to a secluded area of the park where she flops onto the grass with a book.

Without giving it a second thought, I approach her. "What are you reading?"

Startled, she whips her head around and then demands, disbelievingly, "Did you follow me?"

"Yes. What are you reading?"

"Nothing." She tries to snatch it closed, but I bend down and seize it from her grip.

I make a face as I say the title, "*Renaissance*... Oh god, you're boring!"

"If I'm so boring, then what are you doing here? Give it back!"

"Okay, okay... I'm sorry! I didn't really mean that you were boring," I concede.

She glares at me as I throw my backpack onto the grass and sit down next to her.

"Tell me more about Cesare, Kinsey." Her story has me curious.

She gives me a doubtful look. "You want to know?"

"Well, he sleeps with his sister. That's a dirty story!"

She giggles and relaxes a bit. Her smile brings my attention to her pretty dimples.

"Do you want to hear the decent or the twisted?" she asks with a playful grin.

"Hmmm... The twisted." I smile and wink at her.

And in the next couple of hours, Kinsey teaches me more useless facts about the *Renaissance* than any other boy my age will ever know. Time passes as we chat and laugh. She's really cool but seems a bit sad.

I study her as we lie on our backs. "Why do you come here alone?"

She sighs, and just when I think she isn't going to answer, she responds, "Because my father is home. And he's always high on drugs."

"Oh...And your mom?"

"She left a long time ago."

"Oh."

We sit in silence, watching the clouds drift above us.

"Want to come to my house for supper?" I ask, knowing that my mother never minds if I bring a friend home since she always cooks too much food.

"Okay."

And that's how our friendship started. Kinsey had a strange fascination with random historical facts, and she was amusing to be around, unlike the Italian girls I'd grown up with. But being friends with a girl proved to be difficult in the coming years.

CHAPTER 3

Kinsey – present day

"DO YOU TWO KNOW EACH other?" The Italian man named Michael demands to know.

"Yes," Cesare retorts as his caramel eyes pierce through me.

All these men are in designer suits similar to Cesare's. Add that to the shooting and the method of questioning, and I know exactly where I am: with the New York Syndicate.

Cesare and Michael radiate authority, and every woman around me is shivering in terror. My surroundings seem unreal as the stench of blood and gunpowder infuses the air.

"How?" Michael barks.

"She's *my* Kinsey," Cesare explains.

So, Cesare has talked about me to Michael?

"And, Joey, how do *you* know her?" Michael settles his scowl on him.

"We met at a cafe a couple of days ago."

Cesare rakes his dark, wavy hair back with an obviously frustrated swipe of his hand.

I can't seem to tear my gaze from him, and my heart hurts to see him after so long. In his tailor-made suit that doesn't hide his muscular physique, he's no longer the boy I loved. And he's grown more handsome with age. Though, with his beard and strands of longer hair that end just below his ear, he seems harsher as well. Yet he's still as enticing as ever. I'd resigned myself to the idea of never seeing him again and am completely blindsided.

"I need to talk to Kinsey," Cesare announces and hauls me by my upper arm to the hallway and into the first bedroom.

Slightly intoxicated, I'm finally catching up to the fact that I'm in serious trouble.

"So, you're fucking my captain?" Cesare hisses.

The hostility vibrating off him is excruciatingly palpable. Nonetheless, apart from fear, I feel a rising strength. After five years, he can't even manage a hello?

"That's none of your business."

He takes a menacing step closer. "It became my business when you came to this party."

I try to get my bearings, but having him this close is wreaking havoc on my brain. His familiar ocean cologne brings back memories better left in some distant, dusty corner of my mind.

"Jesus Christ, Kins! What are you doing here?" he stresses.

"I-I...*shit*! I'm just friends with Joey, and he invited me to this..."—I wave my hand around—"...this massacre."

"How did you meet Joey?"

"In a cafe. Cesare..."

When I say his name out loud, it's as if we finally realize that we're really, truly standing in front of each other. Cesare edges closer, his breath fans my cheek, and my hand rests on his chest on its own volition. In reaction, he covers my palm with his, and electricity pulses from the heat of his skin.

"Kins," he whispers in an anguished tone and braces my neck, pulling me to him.

I inhale sharply as he nuzzles me – just like he used to do. And it causes the reality of how I ache from his absence in my life to rise to the surface. My entire body is drawn to him as if time hasn't altered our feelings.

I remember the words he said to me so many years ago: *I'll take care of you now.*

But then he moves back, shaking his head and releasing my hand. Rubbing his beard incessantly, he holds my gaze. "What happened to you? You look different, not like *you*."

"I *am* different. Five years have passed; I've changed."

"I guess..."

"What's going to happen now?" I ask.

Cesare merely studies me while he's seemingly lost in thought. Abruptly, he orders me, "Don't talk to anyone! Only answer questions from Michael."

"What? Why? Are you keeping me here?" Frantically, I close the distance between us, but he retreats as if he can't stand to be close to me.

Before he exits the room, he tells me bitterly, "Kinsey, just do as I say or..."

Cesare lets the threat linger, and I swallow. He's fuming, although his eerily calm façade hides it, but I can see his nostrils flaring. My best choice is to comply, so I nod, unsure of his intention. There's so much I want to say, but I can't because the circumstances of our reunion are clouded by murder and death.

Without another word, he opens the door and beckons for me to follow him.

Back in the spacious living room, I notice fewer people. Men are already clearing out dead bodies.

Cesare barks, "Where's Michael?!"

"He's putting Rachel in his room," Joey replies, sneering at me when Cesare looks away.

I simply ignore him and stand there uneasily. *This is so surreal.*

Michael returns and passes me, going to Cesare. They whisper back and forth.

Then Michael points to five girls and me. "You're staying here until I've done a background check. If I find out any one of you is involved with the raid and my fiancée's murder, you won't leave this place alive!"

"You can't just keep us here!" I protest without thinking.

Cesare throws me an icy glare, silently ordering me to zip it.

Michael insolently cocks his head and states, "Do as I say, or I'll show you things worse than death."

His words effectively shut me up as a shiver runs down my spine, and a man with a heavy Italian accent grabs my bicep. "Walk."

I pull my arm back, but Cesare's on the Italian within seconds, shoving him away from me.

"No one touches this girl!" And he sends a damning glare around the room, finally resting it on Michael, who makes an almost imperceptible hand movement. It's as if they're wordlessly communicating.

"Cesare," Joey says. "She's *my* date. What are you doing?"

"Are you questioning my authority?" Cesare snarls.

A gasp comes from the other men.

"No! But...who's she to you?"

Michael and Cesare look at each other again, and Cesare visibly changes.

"Who's she to me?" He gives me a sidelong glance. "I took her virginity."

"You ass!" I retort, unable to hold it back.

And Cesare smirks, dispelling the tension among his men. Hurriedly, Cesare drags me with him, back to the room, and practically throws me onto the bed.

"You're staying here tonight."

Before I get the chance to react, he slams the door closed and locks it from the outside while I bang my palms on the surface. "Cesare?!"

But he's already gone, and I'm trapped in here. Then it dawns on me that he isn't the Cesare that I used to know, yet he is. He was always protective of me, beyond reason, just as he's been today, but the years have hardened him. I guess Cesare must've become a very high-ranking member of the Syndicate.

Sitting down on the edge of the mattress, I wait while our past invades my thoughts.

CHAPTER 4

Kinsey – 11 years ago – age 16

CESARE HAS BEEN MY best friend for four years, but lately, there's a difference. I'm constantly aware when he touches me, and I'm also quite aware of how cute he is. Other girls in school always giggle and flirt with him, and recently, I've started to resent it. But I haven't said anything to him about it, and unfortunately, it's resulted in a distance between us. While I used to see him almost three times a week, now, I sometimes don't speak to him for days.

On occasion, I wonder if he's getting more involved with his father's gang. I've learned that Cesare's father is part of the New York Syndicate, and I understand that their wealth comes from the *Cosa Nostra*, from the criminal world. And Cesare knows about his father too, but he says he isn't part of that life – yet.

Today after school, I'm in the park, lying on my back and reading, when Cesare joins me.

"Hey, *piccolina*."

Because I'm still only 5'4" and my body refuses to grow, he calls me *piccolina*, which is Italian for *shortie*.

Cesare plops down sideways, resting his head on my belly, and takes the book from my hands so that I'll look him in the eye. "Want to hang out tonight?" He tosses my book on the ground and turns onto his stomach, now resting his chin playfully on my belly.

He's so striking, and I fight the urge to wind my fingers in his dark, thick hair that constantly falls over his forehead with strands that never stay in place.

While I want to meet him tonight, I'm otherwise occupied. "I can't."

He perks a brow. "What are you doing?"

"I have a date," I comment softly.

Cesare sits up instantly, and I follow suit so that he doesn't tower over me.

"A date?" he repeats skeptically.

"Yes, a date." It *is* actually my first date, so Cesare's surprised reaction isn't odd.

"With who?" A vein in his forehead throbs, and tension coils his body.

"Are you angry? You go on dates all the time, and then you tell me about them in great detail. I need to date too. I'm almost sixteen, and I haven't even been kissed; it's pathetic. I'm this close to hiring a male escort!" I hold my thumb and forefinger an inch apart and grin.

He barks out a laugh, but the moment of fun is gone as soon as it came, and he quietly murmurs, "I miss you."

"We can hang out tomorrow?"

"Why aren't you answering my question?"

At first, I'm confused, but then I state, "Oh, my date is Parker."

"I fucking hate him!" Cesare snarls.

And I'm surprised by his response. Could he feel the same pull between us? He can have any girl, but could he be attracted to me?

I need to know, so I prompt, "Why are you so mad? Is...Do you not want me to go?"

His gaze snaps to me as he considers his answer. "If you want to go, you can. Just be careful."

I can? And wow, did I just entirely misread this situation.

"I can?" I spit and rise. "I don't need your permission! Just be a friend and support me. Tell me to have fun, like I have over and over while you go on dates with every skank in school!"

Cesare looks as if I've slapped him and grits his teeth. Instead of taking me on, he stands up and strides away without a word.

So I go home to get ready for my date and, hopefully, a first kiss. Even though it's not with the boy I wanted, I'm still nervous. I've waited long enough for Cesare to kiss me, and I'm done waiting.

CHAPTER 5

Cesare – 11 years ago – age 16

I FIND MYSELF STALKING Kins because I can't stand it that she's on a date. I know she only sees me as a brother, but I sure as hell don't see her as my sister. While I've grown to almost six feet, Kinsey's still just as tiny, although, her body and face have changed. Her hips and ass have filled out, and her full, pink lips always tantalize me. My hormones are in overdrive, and I've been having dreams about her. When I've kissed other girls, she's popped up behind my eyelids. I want to kiss *her*. Touch her bare, smooth, bronze skin. Sift my hands through her long black hair. Taste her. Fuck her.

"Fuck!" I hiss out loud in anger.

I should've told her not to go. My entire being repels the idea of Parker dancing with her and touching her. Therefore, I'm now at Bar 50 – the bar that allows minors – following Parker to the men's room.

Before he steps inside, a friend fist-bumps him and says, "Fucking Kinsey tonight, Parker?!"

"That's the plan."

"Good going! Another virgin for you."

This is why I hate Parker. He's an entitled asshole, and he hides it well. I trail him to the bathroom and into the stall.

"What the fuck?!" he shrieks.

Quickly, I close and lock the door and push him down onto the toilet.

"Cesare! Fuck!"

He knows exactly why I'm here and tries to jump up, so I punch him in the nose.

"I believe I was clear when I said that Kinsey was off-limits," I snarl, grabbing him by his collar.

"I wasn't really going to fuck her, man."

"No, you're not. If I ever see you near her again, I'll cut your throat."

His bottom lip trembles. "Shit. Sorry, man. I'll stay away." And he holds up both palms, so I instantly release him, causing him to fall back onto the toilet.

Then I unlock the door, wash my hands, and go to Kins.

Perched on a stool, she's smoking hot in her tight jeans that hug her delectable round ass and a golden top that's tied behind her neck. Kinsey always says that she's so tiny that no one sees her, but she's completely wrong. *I* see her. I see only her. I know that beneath that stunning girl is an even more beautiful soul.

Resting my hands on the bar, I cage her in from behind.

She turns her head so fast that she bumps my nose as I bend down.

"Ouch!" she rubs her nose cutely and frowns.

"Hey, Kins. I'm sorry about earlier." I press my chest against her back, and she sighs.

She leans back toward me as I straighten so that her head falls against my chest.

"Apology accepted."

My palms rake down her bare arms, and I feel her shiver when I press a kiss to the top of her head.

"What are we doing, Cesare? I'm here with Parker." She swivels around on the stool, breaking our intimate contact.

"He left."

"What? How do you know?" She glances around the bar.

"He was talking shit about you. And you were right. I don't want you to be on this date."

"Why not?"

"Because I can't allow other guys to touch you."

A tentative smile tugs at her lips. "So…?"

"So…um—"

"Cesare!" A blonde cheerleader from another school interrupts me, touching my arm.

"Who are you?" I ask, annoyed.

"I've heard about you. You dated my friend…" Then she glances at Kins. "Oh, hey, you must be his sister?"

Kinsey lifts a brow, glowering at her.

Before she answers, I say, "Yes."

And Kins shoots me a stunned, hurt look, then starts to turn around, but I stop her stool and hold it.

"Please leave. I need to talk to my sister." I stare at Kins and smirk, stepping closer to her.

The girl eyes our pose and hurries away to her friends at the other end of the bar.

I entwine our hands and tug her to the dance floor while the group of girls keep their attention focused on us.

"Want to shock them?" I suggest.

"What did you have in mind?" she probes with mischievous eyes.

I pull her body flush to mine and lock my arms around her middle, bending my head so we're face-to-face, trapped in a cocoon of our own. "I'm Cesare, and you're Lucrezia, and we're having a very sordid affair."

"An incest scandal?" She bites her lips playfully and twines her arms around my neck, pressing her breasts against my chest, and my blood flows south furiously.

"Let's dirty dance," I whisper.

And I sway Kinsey to the music. It feels like home to finally have the right girl in my arms. She pulls back, giving me a radiant smile. Kins feels it too, and an explicable sense of satisfaction warms me. Then everything around us shifts. Charges. Music fades into nothingness, and suddenly, we're at a life changing moment.

Nuzzling Kinsey, I brush my lips across hers while my hands drift down to her ass. And then I crush my mouth to hers. My cock stirs when I coax her lips open and delve inside. With our bodies pressed together, we're tasting and touching.

Out of breath, I pull back and rest my forehead against hers. "Your lips are so soft," I utter.

"So are yours."

That makes me groan.

"What?"

"I don't want to hear how any part of me is soft at this moment," I say.

The corner of her mouth tilts up, just slightly, and it makes her even more beautiful. "I'm sorry."

I merely look at her, taking in all her features. How her eyes slant up a little at the corners, enhancing her exotic looks.

She glances behind my shoulder and laughs. The group of girls is staring at us in horror.

I chuckle too. "My Lucrezia, I'm going to kiss you again."

Eagerly, I cradle her head and press my mouth against hers. She excitedly responds, and I need to be alone with her.

"Let's go."

"Yes, please," she says as I twine our fingers and head out to my BMW.

WE'RE CONTENTEDLY LYING on the grass in our spot in the park, Kinsey next to me, her head on my chest as I sift her bangs from her forehead.

"Cesare?"

"Yes?"

"Am I your girlfriend now?"

My movement in her hair stops, and she lifts her head.

"Of course you are," I throw back. "What did you think? You're *mine* now."

She hesitates to voice her next statement. "Don't be mad. I'm not the first girl you've kissed and haven't dated afterward. I just needed to know."

My god, she always knows how to make me feel good and calm. I love that about her.

I tangle my hand in her hair. "You *are* my girlfriend. And you'll be my first in everything else because I promise you, we'll be doing a lot more than kissing real soon." Lightning-fast, I surprise her by grabbing her hips and lifting her to sit astride me. "Feel how hard I am for you. Because you're so hot and delicious, I want to eat you."

"Like...take a bite?"

I bark out a laugh. "No. I want to eat your pussy, *piccolina*. Lick you down there."

Kinsey's brows hit her hairline. "Um..."

"It's going to happen, baby." And I pull her forward to kiss her pretty mouth.

"I'm so horny," I groan into her neck as she sits atop me.

Slowly, she rears back with an expectant gleam in her eyes. "Is there...anything we can do?"

Now it's my turn to be surprised. "Yes. You can touch me."

She slides down a bit as I unfasten my jeans, and she wraps her fingers around my cock.

Her tentative touch is absolutely enthralling to me, and I stiffen within seconds. Covering her hand with mine, I show her how to move.

It's so hot to watch her jerking me off, and then I almost shoot my load when she asks, "Can I taste?"

A growl escapes me. "Woman, you're going to be the death of me. Yes!"

Sweetly, she kisses the head of my cock and wraps her lips around me while pumping the base. I twist my hand in her hair and let my head fall back to the ground as my balls tighten when I guide her head.

"Watch your teeth," I warn and release a growl of pleasure.

My harsh breathing fills the night, and I grunt as I come inside her mouth.

She swallows and slinks back up into my arms with a smile. In comfortable silence, we view a starry sky.

CHAPTER 6
Kinsey – present

A DISTRESSING, SLEEPLESS night passes. No one has entered my room, but I've heard a lot of commotion the last few hours, recognizing Michael's thunderous voice.

After I've washed in the adjacent bathroom, Cesare returns looking clean in his tailored charcoal suit but with dark circles around his eyes that betray his weariness.

"Kinsey, now that I've had some time to think, I need you to answer my questions." He closes the door behind him.

"Okay…" A tremor of angst slithers across my skin.

"How did you get involved with Joey?"

"I've told you; I barely know him."

"But *I* know *you*, and he doesn't seem like the crowd you'd hang out with."

He's wrong. "You don't know me anymore. We haven't been friends for five years. I've changed."

He gives me a derisive glance. "I see that."

"What's that supposed to mean?!" I cock my head.

He ignores my question and bridges the distance between us, swift and smooth, and my heart gives a treacherous thump.

"Trust me; I know you." His knuckles trace down my cheek in a feather light caress that's almost no touch at all, yet it scorches my flesh, and I gasp. Then he palms my neck and rests his forehead against mine. "One look, one touch, and I feel what you feel, Kinsey. You were mine for ten years. I've known your mind since you were twelve, and I can read you like no one else can. You broke my heart, and you ignored me for five years to come waltzing back into my life like this."

"I think we broke each other," I counter. "And you don't know me anymore."

He set our break in motion, and I worsened it by giving up, which is the one regret I have in my life.

Our gazes lock; a battle of wills. But focusing is impossible when he forces memories back to the forefront of my mind.

Mi prenderò cura di te adesso. I'll take care of you now.

"Don't tell me that I don't know you anymore! I've been inside you, and I never left. If I kissed you, you wouldn't deny me!"

His arrogance baffles me, so I push him away. "Who *are* you? Stop playing games. I just want to leave here!"

"I am Cesare, the underboss of the New York Syndicate, and you're not going anywhere," he comments with his back to me and then orders me to walk.

Back in the living room, I'm astounded at the cleaned-up crime scene. The entire place is spotless. And along with a few men and the other women, who apparently slept chained together while I was in the bedroom, I'm lined up again.

My gaze flies to Cesare, but he's in a heated conversation with Michael before he addresses us.

With his gun dangling in his hand, Michael paces back and forth. "My fiancée was killed. In my own home! I want to know which one of you allowed an enemy past the gate, into *my* house, to execute a meaningless raid that not only got them killed, but also got my fiancée killed! We're doing background checks as we speak, but if you come forward now, perhaps I'll be lenient." He aims a quelling glare at us.

Cesare's analyzing me with a mixture of pity and anger. As if he wants to hold me but also throttle me. Then he breaks our stare and resumes his dominant stance.

No one utters a word.

A man comes up behind Michael and whispers to him. Michael pins the guy to my left with a scowl and then points his gun at him.

I feel dizzy but keep standing, my hands sweating profusely and my skin itching.

"Come here. I'm not in the mood for games. You didn't tell me your last cocaine drop-off went sour. Why?" Michael demands.

"We had the problem under control," the man answers shakily.

"So, you lied to me?"

"No, I omitted—"

Michael cocks his weapon and shoots him right between the eyes; the body sags to the floor. "Anyone who lies to me gets executed on the spot!"

The women scream, and the other men seem astounded as well.

Cesare is impossible to read, but he says something to Michael, and they leave.

Joey is on me the next second. "What did you tell Cesare? I didn't know you fucking knew Cesare Amallo! If he finds out, I'm dead."

"Then I guess you better get me out of here or get me a fix real soon because I'm dying from withdrawal."

I'm a mess, having sweat all night from withdrawal, and I've completely lost my grip on myself due to Cesare. Seeing him pains me. And I need the pain to fade. I need drugs to erase years of regret, of missing my best friend, my one love who doesn't want me anymore.

No! I don't need the drugs!

I've been fighting for months to get clean, but Joey feeds my addiction. I know he's bad news, and I should've stayed away from him – then I wouldn't have ended up in this mess – but I'm an addict without funds. I have no job, student loans to pay off, and I keep falling back into his clutches. I run drugs for him in secret, and he pays me in heroine.

Sometimes, in lucid moments, I can't believe what's become of me, and I try to get clean, but I've failed repeatedly. However, in this moment, I grasp how far gone I really am. I've witnessed a massacre and am being held hostage, but all I can think about is getting a fix. This is horrific, and I don't want any of it.

My musings are interrupted when Cesare smacks Joey's hand away from my arm.

"Do not *ever* touch her again," he spits, and Joey holds up both palms as Cesare drags me back to the bedroom.

"I don't know what you're playing at, or how the hell you got involved with Joey, but you don't want me to find out from anyone else. I'll be back tonight, and I expect you to have answers for me."

Then he locks me in again while I'm already considering confessing. Even though Cesare is different, there's still this pull between us. Why else would he be putting me in a room instead of leaving me with the others? He's just as affected by our reunion as I am. Maybe I should confide in him? He's still my friend, my first and only love. And a love as deep as ours never fades.

CHAPTER 7

Kinsey – 11 years ago – age 16

THAT FIRST KISS IS the game changer. Cesare and I become thick as thieves in the next few months, and my crush on him evolves into my first love. When I'm not with him, I miss him desperately.

Unfortunately, he has a problem with my father and the crappy part of town I live in, so Cesare picks me up in the middle of the night so I can sleep at his house.

Tonight, I jump out my bedroom window and head toward Cesare's car.

"Wow! You look beautiful, Kins!"

"Thanks."

He takes my hand and entwines our fingers as he pulls out onto the road and drives us to his home, a beautiful brownstone in the heart of the city.

TWENTY MINUTES LATER, I'm on his bed, kissing him. Already in just my panties and bra, I'm lying underneath an almost naked Cesare. Our ragged breathing fills the room as he pushes his erection between my legs, a layer of clothing preventing skin-to-skin contact.

"Kins, I want to be inside you," he growls, caressing his fingertips down my cheek, and I nod.

He shows me a lopsided boyish grin, roaming his hands all over my body.

"You're so beautiful, *piccolina*," he murmurs as he unhooks my bra and sucks my nipples.

Arching off the bed, I feel a tingling responsiveness in my lower stomach as Cesare nips a path down my stomach and legs, removing my panties and spreading me wide.

Then he lies between my legs, his mouth close to my core. "I'm going to taste you now."

As he kisses me there, I grab his hair in surprise, but it feels amazing when he starts to lick and suck.

"Cesare..." I moan.

He looks up. "Does it feel good, Kins?"

I smile, and he continues enthusiastically. Sensations I've never experienced shake my body as he devours me. Harder and rougher. I reach for ultimate bliss and peak when I gaze down and see him lying between my legs. It seems so forbidden, and I pant while pushing my hips from the bed.

While I'm still shivering in the aftermath, Cesare climbs up my body and gets rid of his boxer briefs.

"That was hot," Cesare whispers and crushes his mouth to mine, rubbing his hard-on against my center.

He rests his forearms beside my head, fingers weaving into my hair. And we stare at each other as he starts to enter me.

I flinch from the pain, and he strokes my hair. "Shhh..."

He pushes through, and it hurts, but he smothers me with a kiss and slowly thrusts. Gradually, I'm adjusting to the fullness.

Then I notice that Cesare's shaking. "Cesare..."

Our gazes lock.

"You feel so warm, Kins. It's so wet."

I let the tips of my fingers caress down his back and urge him to keep going.

He drives inside of me while studying my face intently. "Are you okay?"

"Yes. Please, don't stop."

And he picks up his pace. I welcome him into my body, and the pain transforms to a dull ache that quickly dwindles. Touching Cesare's lips, I lock eyes with him while we move together, my nipples brushing his chest, and I've never felt closer to anyone.

"Fuck! Kins, I'm going to come," he groans and drops his head into my neck as he pushes in deep.

Then he collapses on top of me while I rub his back. His harsh breathing settles, and he shifts off me, rolling me to my side to face him. I touch his pecs as he strokes my hips.

"I can't believe we did it," I utter with a smile.

He laughs, a truly happy laugh. "That's the first thing you say after our first time?" Quickly, he rolls me onto my back again. "You always surprise me." And he pulls back.

Satisfied, we just lie in silence, enjoying the moment to its fullest.

"*Piccolina...*"

I know what he's going to say because I feel it too.

"*Ti amo*. I love you."

"I love you too."

Something in me is different, altered. Maybe I'm tied to Cesare forever now? The boy I've loved for so long, who would become my first everything in the next couple of years.

CHAPTER 8

Cesare – 9 years ago – age 18

FOR THE NEXT TWO YEARS, Kinsey and I are inseparable. She's my confidant, my lover, my home, *mine*.

However, change is upon us. We're in my bedroom when she drops a bomb on me.

"Cesare, I got accepted to Chicago State, to study history," she mentions, sitting on my bed Indian style.

"Why? Can't you study history here? At NYU?"

She gives me a solemn look. "I can't afford that."

"Then I'll pay for it." I'll be at Princeton, which is like a three-hour flight from Chicago, and I don't want to be that far away from her.

"How?"

"I don't know; I'll ask my parents. I have a fund I could use."

"That's really sweet, but you can't. And I couldn't take it anyway. It's way too much. I'd rather stay here with you too, but we don't have a choice."

I get up from my chair and go to the bed. "I don't like this, *piccolina*. We see each other every day."

She takes my hand in hers. "I'm going to miss you so much, but we'll call and text. And you can come visit me?"

"Won't you visit me?"

She sighs and averts her gaze.

"I meant that if I buy you a ticket, will you come? I know you don't have the money, but you will accept that, right?"

"Of course. I love you, and I don't want all of this."

"Me either." I hug her.

A sense of foreboding settles in my soul, and suddenly, I'm dreading the future.

ON EDGE, I FIND MYSELF in my car outside Kins's house watching over her.

Her father returns home at three a.m., and I can see through the window that Kinsey has been waiting up for him. She turns on the lights, so I get out of the vehicle to ensure that she's safe.

As I approach the front door of the tiny one-story, I hear them arguing inside.

"Where have you been? You come home totally spaced out after being gone for days! I've been worried sick about you!" she scolds her father.

"Kinsey, calm down and go to bed," he slurs, sitting on the couch as I peek through the window.

"No! Not this time. I always let you get away with everything. But now, you've gone too far. You stole my money!"

Motherfucker! He stole her hard-earned money that she's been saving for Chicago for drugs?

"I said *go to bed*!" her father roars. "I'm getting sick and tired of your sanctimonious bitching, girl!"

My blood boils with the way her father treats her.

Kinsey has reached her breaking point, because she starts to shout, "I want my money back!"

"Do not yell! This is still my house!"

Seeing her father striding to Kins, ready to strike her, I race back to the front door, but it's locked.

"Kinsey!!" I shout and hurl my entire body against it repeatedly.

All of a sudden, I hear her piercing scream and a loud commotion.

"Kins!!" Panic fills my veins with my need to protect her. So with all my strength, I drive my shoulder against the door, breaking its hinges.

I run inside to seize her father, who's slapping Kinsey's cheeks while she's lying on her back on the floor, and a red haze overtakes my vision.

She's hurt. An animalistic rage courses through me; no one hurts what's mine.

Kinsey is blocking her face with her forearms, struggling, when I throw him off her.

He grunts in pain as he sags against the wall. Then he lunges up and comes at me with all his force. His weight crushes the air from my lungs, and he punches me. In turn, I strike him in his nose with my fist.

"Cesare!" she shouts.

"Kins, run! Go!" I order frantically.

Instead, she jumps on her father, and he shoots to the side, flinging her off. Kins hits her head on the floor and cries in pain.

"Kinsey! No!"

She's not moving when her father bends down and smiles maliciously, now flashing a knife in his hand. Then he jumps on me again, and we topple to the floor, everything after that happening fast. I fight him, trying to take the weapon, and grunt when he knees me in the stomach. Then he lifts his hand, ready to stab me, but I catch his wrist, roll over, and with all my power, take the knife and plunge it into his heart.

"Motherfucker!" I bellow.

He bucks and spits blood, convulsing while I hurry to Kins.

"Kinsey!" I lift her onto my lap, cradling her head.

Her eyes open languidly as blood trails down her ear.

Anxiously, I ask, "Are you okay?"

"My heart hurts...that's all." She touches my cheek. "You?"

"I'm okay. But we need help, *piccolina*."

She sits up and stares at the body of her father.

"Oh, my god! Is he...?"

"I think so." I rise to my feet and plow my hand through my hair.

Serenity returns to my system now that I know she's okay, but we have a huge problem at the moment. And there's only one person who can help me.

Fishing my phone from my pocket, I make the call. "I need a clean-up crew."

Unfortunately, Kinsey's father's death will tie me to the Syndicate forever – much earlier than initially planned.

HALF AN HOUR LATER, I'm on the porch with a distraught Kinsey, who's in shock, while members of the New York Syndicate clean the house and dispose of the body.

Luciano, my father and the Syndicate's counselor and lawyer, arrives, scowling at me. But his face softens when he witnesses Kinsey's sad state.

"You involved the Syndicate in your business, son. You'll go with me tomorrow to explain this to the boss. I didn't want you to become part of this so soon, but it's done now. Come. Let's go. Your mother's worried."

With Kinsey in my arms, I head to my car to take us home.

In the vehicle, Kinsey calms my soul. "I love you, Cesare."

She loves a killer? I'm a killer, about to become a soldier for the NYS, and within years, I'll be a *made man*. She doesn't realize how this will dramatically change our lives.

Still, I seek to give her peace, so I kiss the back of her hand. "I love you too, *piccolina*. Everything will be okay. *Mi prenderò cura di te adesso*. I'll take care of you now."

Regrettably, little do I know that my promise will be impossible to uphold.

RIGHT BEFORE I GO OFF to college, my parents reveal their objections to our relationship for the first time. My father especially doesn't like it because he can sense that she's pulling me away from the mafia life I'm supposed to initiate into after Princeton. But for now, I don't think about that. I'm happy with Kins, and we'll make it.

Tonight, my father awaits me in my room. "Cesare, we need to talk."

Uh-oh, that's never good. I hurl my keys onto the desk. "About what, father?"

"You and Kinsey."

"Why?"

"I think you and she are very close and much too young to practically be shacking up together in your room."

"She's my girlfriend, and she's doesn't have anyone else. You know that."

"I do. And I applaud you for taking care of her, but that's not your responsibility. Don't forget that you and she come from different worlds. You need to enjoy your teenage years, son. And after college, you will initiate. Does she know that?"

"No, but she'll follow me anywhere. Don't worry about her."

"I don't worry about her. I worry about you two together. Cesare, when she's here, you neglect your friends and you're always obsessed with being with her. I'm warning you, don't let her become your weakness."

My father's concerned tone upsets me. I know he means well, and we've never argued, but Kinsey's a topic that's non-negotiable to me.

"She won't," I manage to grind out, which belies my statement entirely.

My father studies me, but lets it go and calmly leaves my room.

CHAPTER 9

Kinsey – 9 years ago – age 18

TIME PASSES QUICKLY. After my father's death, I feel liberated, and Cesare and I are madly in love in the months before I leave. Nevertheless, there's always a feeling of desperation in our relationship because of our impending separation.

Cesare and I share a joyless goodbye when I leave for college. We have high hopes that we can make a long-distance relationship work, but sometimes good intentions aren't enough.

I've missed him terribly, but as life continues, he's become less approachable. His Syndicate life and college are eating up all his time. We've drifted apart in physical distance and spiritual distance as well. It's taken five months for him to even come to visit me.

In my scant room on campus, we can't take it slow.

"Kins, I've missed you. My cock needs to be inside you." Cesare kisses me roughly and slams me back against the wall.

My skirt is bunched up while I unfasten his slacks and pump his erection. He swells rapidly in my hands. No time to undress, I want to feel him in me.

He spins me around, his chest against my back, nudges my panties aside, and drives into me. I gasp, and Cesare grips my hips, fucking me from behind as I arch my back to take him in deep. Whimpering, I push back against him while he ruthlessly possesses me and groans into my ear. His hand drifts to my center and rubs me as he pistons inside. And I explode, riding the tide of pleasure in irresistible waves. He growls while slowing his punishing pace and drops his forehead on my shoulder.

After our breathing has calmed, we move to lie on my bed, and I notice his tousled state. He has dark circles around his eyes and looks like he hasn't shaved in weeks.

"Cesare, you look…"

"Tired? I am tired." He pulls me into his embrace and kisses my head. "But I'm better now that we're together."

I didn't want to say *tired*. No, he looks different. Hardened, perhaps?

However, we're going to be together for a few days, and when we're together, everything's perfect.

After that, we continued to see each other every couple of months. Still, as the years passed, Cesare changed more, and so did I, and when we were apart, we were a mess.

CHAPTER 10
Cesare – 6 years ago – age 21

MY THIRD YEAR IN COLLEGE, the fifth year into my relationship with Kinsey, I realize that our bond has been tainted by our miles apart.

My life has become one of drugs and murder. I'm getting more and more immersed in the mayhem of the underworld. And my calmness, my home, has been living so far away for years. I'm starting to resent Kinsey and my love for her. I miss her so much that I ache and find solace in cocaine. We fight when we're apart, and we love obsessively during the few days every couple of months we see one another.

We rarely make love anymore. No, we fuck. During this time, we have rough and hard sex when we meet. Maybe it's due to the pent-up frustration of being away from each other, especially since we know that if we were together, we'd be happy. The distance is killing us, and that same distance, combined with being a prospect in the Syndicate, makes one lonely. And choices made out of loneliness usually lead to the biggest mistakes. Moreover, drugs combined with loneliness can be lethal. And my solitude, and all the toxic things that came with it, was the catalyst for my creating the first cracks in our love.

CHAPTER 11

Kinsey - 5 years ago – age 22

DURING OUR COLLEGE years, Cesare breaks my heart twice. The first time, I forgive him, but after the second time, I've had enough of his indiscretions.

I'm at his dorm the first day of my visit. We had a falling out because I think he's been doing drugs: he looks terrible. And then he left and has been gone for hours.

When he returns, I know something bad has happened; he's been slowly slipping away from me for years.

His red-rimmed eyes plead with me before he's even opened his mouth.

"What's wrong with you? You just disappear when I've flown three hours to finally see you again?"

"Kins, I-I need to talk to you about something important." He edges closer and I step back.

"Just spit it out."

"I made a huge mistake." He studies me intently, and moisture wells in his eyes.

Time stops as my heartbeat pounds in my chest. "Just say it. What did you do?!"

"I was drunk and high. I..." He averts his gaze.

"Tell me!"

"I slept with someone else. I'm so sorry! It meant nothing!" He strides to me and cups my face. "It was a mistake."

My heart shatters into a million pieces – again. Last year, he kissed another girl when he was pissed, but this is *so* much worse.

I shake my head and push him away forcefully. "Don't you fucking touch me! When did it happen?!"

"A couple of weeks ago. I've been feeling like shit, and I missed you so much. I...I was weak."

The trust we've built for almost six years obliterates in that moment. A hole forms inside of me, and I feel empty.

"Kins, please say something," he begs, watching me closely.

I merely stare at the floor. "Who is she?"

"No one. She means nothing."

"That doesn't make me feel better right now," I counter sadly and catch his gaze. "I'm going home."

"No!" He blocks my path at the door after I've swung my bag over my shoulder.

"I want to talk." He holds up both hands. "Kinsey, please stay. We need to talk!"

"Get out of my way."

"Fine. I'll leave, and you call me when I can come back and you're ready to talk."

I grit my teeth but know he won't budge, so I nod.

Reluctantly, he goes.

After five minutes, I check the hall and leave.

Cesare rounds the corner. Of course, he was checking on me.

I hurry along to the entrance of the dorm as he screams my name, but a guy blocks his path, so I run outside to hail the first cab I see.

"To the airport," I say and go home, where I crawl into my bed and sit with my knees drawn up to my chest and my face buried in my hands. I hurt too much to even cry, and I shake so badly that my teeth are chattering.

I'M IN A ROBOTIC STATE for the next few weeks. Going to classes, taking exams, and dodging Cesare's calls. I've texted him once that I'll contact him when I'm ready, but I'm coming to the realization that we might've reached our final destination. I can't trust Cesare anymore, and I can't be in a relationship where I have to wonder if he's being faithful. The drugs have made him too volatile. The distance has broken us indefinitely.

While I'm alone in my room, someone knocks on my door, and I jump up.

"Kinsey! Open the door. I know you're home!"

Shit! I'm not ready to confront him yet.

"Kinsey!" He pounds the door harder, more furiously. "I'm not leaving until we talk!"

Nervously, I sit on the mattress.

He hits the door again. "I'm fucking dying without you! I'll wait here all night if I have to." Another slam and then he whispers, "Please, don't turn me away."

His broken tone hurts me, and I feel compelled to provide him closure.

But Cesare's unstable mood is scaring me, so I say, "Meet me at the coffee shop across the street. I'll be there in ten minutes."

"Okay."

FIVE MINUTES LATER, I sit across from Cesare in a booth, hearing him apologize for the umpteenth time. I don't even recognize him with his scruffy beard, and I can tell that he's high, which strengthens my resolve to end us.

"I'm so sorry, Kins. I miss you. I lost my home, my lover, my best friend, all on the same day! Please, please give me another chance."

"I've already given you a second chance. I can't do it a third time. Trusting you while you're on drugs is breaking my heart."

"I'm not *on drugs*. I only use occasionally," he defends.

"*You* are still in denial, and I'm done. I'm sorry. You should've known better."

Sadness clouds his face, then ire blisters to the surface. The loss of control is making him angry; this is his harsher side. He's not used to not getting his way.

"I've done everything for you. All of it! This mafia fucking life that I'm in is for you! You will not walk away from me!"

"Don't make this ugly, Cesare. You'll regret it. I'm sorry, but you and I are over. Our foundation of trust is gone; it's been broken. *By you.* I need space now. Maybe in a couple of months, we can be friends again, but right now, I can't see you anymore."

He clenches his jaw as his eyes water. "If you walk away now, it's over for good!"

"Don't do this, Cesare." I slide out from the booth, and he glares at me but stays seated; challenging me.

"Kinsey, I'm serious! Don't leave me!" He grabs my wrist.

"Don't give me ultimatums! *You* broke us! Not *me*. Now leave me alone so I can pick up the pieces of my life." And I wrench free right after I see a tear rolling down his cheek.

That was the last time I saw Cesare. But I was never free of him.

During my time with him, I learned about love. Love is fantastic when it's good. However, when it's bad, it can result in a catastrophe. And after we broke up, I spiraled out of control due to my broken heart.

I did text him a couple of times after that day in the coffee shop, but he never responded. I was left more heartbroken than I could ever imagine, and after graduation, I couldn't find a decent job. Eventually, I ended up living paycheck to paycheck while life persistently continued. I drank, I did drugs, and I fucked around a lot to get over Cesare. But nothing ever helped.

CHAPTER 12

Cesare – 5 years ago – age 22

WHEN SHE WALKED OUT, I knew that I would never feel for another girl what I felt for Kinsey. She would forever be *the one that got away.*

Dejected and furious, I return to New York and to a seething father who sets me straight. He's discovered I've been snorting cocaine, and if I'm to become a member, I need to be clean.

"This is what I warned you about four years ago. You're going to get clean, initiate into the Syndicate, and forget about that girl. She's toxic to you. But enough about her; on to business. Here's your new Syndicate-issued phone." My father takes my old phone while I'm despairing, bitterness consuming my soul.

Kinsey has ripped my heart out, and anger fills the hole she's created.

"Cesare, your love is destructive," my mother adds. "She's not the girl for you. Forget her and move on. You're going to be a *made man.* Act like it."

"I've loved her for almost half my life. How do I let her go?"

"One day at a time, son. Time heals all wounds."

I got clean and became a captain right after graduation. Without Kinsey, I focused solely on the Syndicate. And when Michael became boss, he made me his underboss.

Time might heal all wounds, but time never makes you forget. Women have come and gone throughout the years, but only one holds a place in my heart. And that will never change.

CHAPTER 13

Cesare - present

"MICHAEL, WHAT WAS THAT all about?" I inquire in Michael's office right after he shot the soldier in front of the other women in the living room.

Michael is on the warpath. "That soldier should've informed us. You know that."

"Yes, but why the charade? Last night, you want to scare him, and today, you kill him on the spot. Let the rest leave. Only keep the date of the soldier you just killed, his accomplice. We killed all the men last night and eliminated the leader of the raid. Now, you need to calm down and go focus on saying goodbye to Rachel. Don't waste your energy on drawn out revenge. We killed the ones who killed her. Now, go grieve."

Michael braces his neck forcefully before relaxing. "Fine. Let them leave. I don't understand why you kept them or Kinsey anyway. Do you hate her that much?"

"No, I love her that much. There's something between Kinsey and Joey, and I'm not letting him ruin my third chance with her. If she'd left last night, she would've disappeared. I needed her to think about us for a night. A little manipulation can be quite persuasive. I'm doing it to protect her," I reveal honestly. "I want her back."

His gaze flies to me, astonished. "I always knew you were waiting for her. Every girl you dated had a certain...quality." Michael sighs. "So go; take her back. But Cesare, be prepared to always protect her when she's part of our life."

"I'm ready," I say with conviction.

For five years, I've been living life going through the motions, but Kinsey belongs with me. She's a part of me that I've been missing for too long.

"I failed. I would hate for you to go through what I am now."

"Together, we'll get through it. Go to Rachel, Michael."

My confirmation regarding Joey and Kins's peculiar connection comes when I'm back in the living room, and Joey is manhandling her.

Rushing over, I slam his hands off her.

"Do not *ever* touch her again!" I snarl.

I can't stand not knowing exactly what their association is, and I'm on edge, so I lock her back in the bedroom and order the captains to release the other captives – *if* they can be persuaded into silence. The rest will be killed.

AFTER I FINISH WITH the day's business, I rush back to the mansion to see Kinsey and am confronted with how much she actually needs me.

I unlock the door and frown at the empty room. Then I spot the nightstand's lamp broken on the floor and run to the bed.

"No!"

Kinsey is lying on the floor on the other side of the bed, unconscious.

Rushing over the mattress, I check her pulse, but it's weak.

"Kins! Kins!"

Panic I haven't experienced in years almost renders me incapacitated, then rage overcomes me when I see fresh track marks on the inside of her elbow. Hurriedly, I check her other arm and see more scars.

Unexpectedly, she starts to convulse and bucks, coughing. So I roll her to her side, and she vomits. I keep her in that position until she stops heaving; however, I still can't wake her up.

"No! You're fucking high!" As I sit on the floor, I take her weak body into my arms and hold her tightly while I call the Syndicate doctor.

"I need you at Michael's house. Right now! I've got an overdose!" And the phone slides from my hand, dropping onto the floor with a thud.

While I wait in agonizing silence with her frail body in my arms, moisture wells in my eyes. I can't lose her now that I've finally got her again.

The doctor storms into the room after I don't know how long. I've been incessantly checking her pulse and carefully lay her on the bed. He examines her as I stare down at the love of my life.

"Cesare, she'll wake soon. It's good that you let her vomit or else she would've choked on it. Just keep her on her side until she wakes. And Cesare, from observing several puncture wounds on her arms, I can tell you that she's an addict," he states solemnly. "Who is she?"

"My best friend. You can go. I'll watch over her." I take the chair and sit down.

My best friend is on drugs.

What happened to you, piccolina?

Sadness washes over me, and the realization of how long we've been apart hits me. Life has a funny way of turning out. She left me due to drugs, and in the end, I'm clean and she's an addict.

I never wanted this for you.

A tear streams down while I take her hand in mine, wishing she'd never left me. I won't let this third chance escape my grasp. When she wakes, she must own up.

CHAPTER 14

Kinsey - present

I AWAKE IN AN INSTANT, meeting Cesare's concerned face. He's sitting in a chair next to the bed, studying me, clutching my hand tightly in his. The warmth of his skin seeps into mine, making me feel protected like only he can.

"Welcome back." His voice is low. "How are you feeling?"

"Like crap..."

He smiles tersely. "What happened?"

Cesare leans forward, not letting go of my hand, and I realize it's time to fess up.

"Joey happened. He came in here to give me a fix."

His lips thin into a straight line. "So, Joey's your dealer?"

I nod and avert my gaze to the window.

Cesare is absentmindedly rubbing my hand with his thumb, the touch so pleasurable in its simplicity. The permanent ache in my heart echoes the truth.

How much I've missed him.

Our gazes clash, and he sends me grave look. "How long have you been addicted, Kins?"

My words abandon me at first, yet I power through and confess for the first time that I am an addict, "A year. I try to stop, but it's so hard. And Joey gives me drugs in exchange for runner jobs."

Cesare's eyes narrow, and his fury becomes palpable.

"I asked for a fix, but then I didn't want to take the drugs, so we struggled and he shot me up because he was afraid I'd tell you if I was too lucid."

"You were out cold and started vomiting." He releases my hand harshly and rises. "Is that enough of a warning for you to stop? Does your life mean nothing to you anymore? You could've died!"

"I'm sorry. I've been a little...lost, Cesare. And I miss you – a lot."

He stares down his nose at me, so I sit up. I'm aching and searching for peace in drugs, but I want him. A singular tear streams down my cheek, and he follows the trail with his finger, wiping my hurt away with his thumb first and then with his words, "I miss you too. Why didn't you ever contact me?"

"I did. But after those dozen messages I sent you in the week following our break-up, I gave up."

His brows snap together. "I never got your messages. My father got me a new phone back then. I assume that he or my mother erased your messages on my old phone. I kept it for over six months in hopes that you would forgive me, Kins. Otherwise, I would've answered. I-I...It's killing me to see you like this. You were always this vibrant girl."

"Life got in the way, and I couldn't find a job." My head is starting to pound, and my weakened body is hurting.

The mattress dips as Cesare sits right beside my hip, and I break down.

"I was lonely, Cesare. I'm a drug addict. I ruined my life, and I don't deserve your help, because I left you when the roles were reversed."

He forces my gaze on him by forcefully cupping my cheeks. "You left me, but I never left you. And I *will* never leave you."

"What do you mean?"

"Do you want to be clean?"

"Yes."

"Then we'll do it together. You just need some help, Kins. And I'm here now to help you." He kisses my forehead. "The situation regarding the attack is under control. You're coming with me, and the doctor and I will get you through withdrawal. But"—he looks me in the eye—"no more drugs. *Ever.*"

I nod. "And what about us?"

"It's time I mend the promise I broke; I'll take care of you."

"Cesare, thank you."

"We'll take it one day at a time. You're coming with me, to my house."

I smile because I finally see some light in the darkness I've been living in since I made the wrong choice and used heroine that first time a year ago.

Cesare rises and ominously states, "And Kins, Joey will pay."

CHAPTER 15

Cesare - present

I EXIT THE ELEVATOR into my penthouse apartment with Kinsey's hand entwined with mine.

After the weekly visit to the doctor, we can celebrate her fourth week in recovery. Withdrawal has been hell for her, and my heart's hurt when I've had to hold her trembling and sweating body at night when she craves the heroin. But slowly, she's getting clean. And she's lived with me for over a month, letting me take care of her. Having her back calms my restless soul after five years of feeling incomplete.

"I'm proud of you!" I say as I release her hand and toss my keys onto the coffee table.

"Thank you. I couldn't do this without you, Cesare." She rests both palms on my chest as she stands close in front of me.

Her familiar perfume invades my nostrils, and my dick stands to attention.

"You're very welcome." I grin when she edges closer, and I grasp her hips, pressing my erection against her stomach.

She looks up at me through her lashes and smirks teasingly.

"I think you can tell what I want, *piccolina*."

"I can." She grins and steps back. "You want to know more about Cesare and Lucrezia because you love my tales?!" She smiles with a twinkle in her eyes and then spins around and dashes down the hall to the bedroom.

"You can run, but you can't hide!" I chase her eagerly while laughing.

At the foot of the bed, I catch her waist from behind, pressing her back against me while whispering into her ear, "While I do love your tales, I didn't mean that. And you're obligating me to tell you precisely what I *do* want. I want..." I kiss the sensitive skin behind her ear. "...to eat your pussy until you come all over my tongue. And then my cock needs to be inside you. To fuck you hard and fast."

Kinsey groans and pushes her luscious ass into my aching groin.

"I want to taste you too, Cesare," she says, craning her neck, and I reward her with a kiss, turning her around and crushing my mouth against hers as she unbuckles my pants.

Kinsey kneels and wraps her lips around my cock while pumping the base. Grunting, I grab her hair into a ponytail while moving in and out. Then I trace her lips with the head of my dick, marking what's mine.

Hurriedly, I tug her up and undress her completely, flinging her onto the bed as she shrieks.

"Sit up, Kins."

The corner of her lip tilts up; she knows what I want.

So I lie on my back, and she positions herself on top of me, her knees on either side of my head and her pussy positioned right above my mouth while she's facing my cock.

Hooking my arms around her hips, I devour her.

"Ah, Cesare," she moans as I circle my tongue and hold her hips.

When she takes me into her mouth, her sweet, lashing tongue has me almost coming down her throat. Kins mashes her pussy against my face and whimpers louder and louder, so I thrust a finger inside and suck her clit. My cock is rock-hard while we both lick and suck and groan.

"Fuck, god, your mouth..." I growl and spear her pussy with my tongue.

Kinsey throws her head back while fisting my erection and climaxes in a loud scream as tremors of desire rake her body and I slowly lick her. Needing to release inside her, I turn her to sit astride me.

"Ride me," I order and grab her wrists, pulling her forward.

Her hair curtains us in a world of our own. The world I lost for five years but will never let go of again. I kiss her while she rubs her pussy against the head of my cock, and I push inside her, making her gasp. When her flesh gives and she starts to move up and down, I grip her hips as she rests her palms on my chest. Kinsey's passionate grey eyes meet mine, and my dick swells from being inside the woman who was meant for me.

Before I can say it, she says in a husky voice laced with lust, "I love you."

Sitting up, I cradle the back of her head with one hand while resting the other on her ass, kissing her harshly. "*Ti amo, piccolina.* Ever since I was twelve."

Her arms loop around my neck as she moves her hips faster and faster. She rides me hard, and I suck her nipples as she arches her back and clutches my hair tightly. My balls tighten while pleasure rockets me, and I come inside her sweet pussy, thoroughly depleted.

We sit motionless, locked in an embrace, so close together not even a hairbreadth separates us. And I finally feel complete again.

Kinsey moves off me, and we recline on the bed, her head on my chest while I stroke her hair. Both lost in our thoughts while our breathing calms.

Then she mutters, "It was fate that I was there that night of the raid in Michael's house. Fate brought us back together. Please don't break my heart again."

Tugging her hair, I force her to look at me. "Never. I'm not that boy anymore."

"I know you're not," Kinsey states.

Her kiss-swollen lips curve up, and she stares at me as if she can't believe I'm truly with her. It's a look of devotion that I've missed.

"Do you believe in soulmates, Cesare?" she asks suddenly in a tender tone.

I sift her hair to the side, away from her eyes, and answer honestly, "Yes, ever since the day I met you."

KINSEY IS BACK IN MY life and all is right.

Although, *I* know she realizes I'm the underboss of the most powerful mafia in New York, Michael needs confirmation. But first, I want to give her revenge against Joey because I need her to feel empowered and safe with me.

Kinsey and I enter Michael's house a month after the raid, and my captain already has Joey in the basement, tied to a bar hanging from wall-to-wall.

"Where are we going?" Kinsey probes.

Before I turn the knob, I tell her, "Joey needs to pay for what he did to you." And I open the door.

She doesn't flinch when she sees him. Thankfully, she sees the same man that I do; the man that drugged her. Joey crossed the line when he hurt her, and even though he's a captain, I'm the underboss and outrank him. I only needed permission to capture him from Michael, who gave it happily.

Michael's also present and greets Kinsey while gripping Joey's chin.

He's been in here for weeks, deprived of food and living off water. His emaciated body sways, and his tired eyes are unfocused.

"You..." he whispers, sneering at Kinsey.

Just as I'm about to speak, she amazes me and strides to him, grabbing his hair. "You ruin people. You take vulnerable girls off the streets and use them. You made your biggest mistake when you singled me out. Because"—she glances back over her shoulder at me—"I'm his."

Kinsey and Michael step aside, and a malicious smile curves Michael's lips as I take out my gun from my back waistband.

Joey stutters, "Cesare, please...pl-please. I didn't know she was yours."

"Too little"—I smash the butt of my weapon into his nose—"too late. No one hurts what's mine!"

Handing over my gun to Michael, I clench my fist and hit Joey's face, again and again, relishing in the pain shooting through my knuckles.

Then I hiss while gripping his hair, "I'm going to keep you on the edge of death, bruised and starving, until you pray for the sweet agony of death. I'll deliver your body to your friends to send them a message to run. Everyone who ever gave Kinsey drugs will be hunted and killed."

His head slouches forward when I release him, and blood drips from his chin.

I face Kinsey and hold out my hand for her to accept.

Michael elaborates, "You're affiliated with the New York Syndicate now. You're an accomplice. Do you understand? As Cesare's partner, we will protect you with the extent of our power. But, if *you* ever betray us, *he* will pay with his life. Cesare will be executed."

She swallows, and a nervous chill runs down my spine. However, my anxiety is unfounded because she takes my offered hand and nods.

"Make my underboss happy then," Michael says.

"I will," she replies in a sincere tone.

And we leave a groaning Joey behind to rot.

After exiting the basement, I take Kinsey into my arms, feeling content, and kiss the top of her head. She belongs with me and has accepted all that I am. We don't even need words; our tight embrace says it all. This is the beginning of our forever.

CHAPTER 16
Kinsey - present

IN CESARE'S ARMS, I realize that maybe we're just all broken, and finding the right soulmate makes us whole.

When Cesare and I are with each other, we're good – as always. It just took a drastic event to bring us back together. Sometimes you need to hit rock bottom in order to move on.

It took a total of fifteen years for our love to find its happily ever after. It took four years of friendship, six years of a relationship, and five years of separation for us to understand that a life apart isn't manageable for either of us. Cesare makes me complete. In the past and in the forever future. All of him, including his anarchic Syndicate.

"Now I get to take care of you forever," he whispers into my ear.

I look up at him as he kisses me with a passion that locks him even tighter in my heart. Then he nuzzles me, and I'm home, where I belong.

The end.

Do you want to read full-length illicit & seductive & forbidden romances? Then one-click the *Chicago Syndicate series* now.

Books by Soraya Naomi

CHICAGO SYNDICATE SERIES

For Cesare (Syndicate #0.5) (standalone)

For Fallon (Chicago Syndicate #1)

For Luca (Chicago Syndicate #2)

For Adriano (Chicago Syndicate #3) (standalone)

For Cam (Chicago Syndicate #4) (standalone)

For Logan (Chicago Syndicate #5) (standalone)

Black Hat Hacker (Chicago Syndicate #6) (standalone)

The Lawyer and the Tramp (Chicago Syndicate #7) (standalone)

For the Love of Luca (Chicago Syndicate #8) (standalone)

The Man in Black (Chicago Syndicate #9) (standalone)

For Christiano, With Hate (Chicago Syndicate #10) (standalone in series)

STANDALONE BOOKS

Sins

ABOUT THE AUTHOR

SORAYA NAOMI IS THE author of the Chicago Syndicate mafia series. She writes provocative novels with a sinfully seductive blend of romance, suspense & men who love hard and at all costs. The Chicago Syndicate series – #1 Amazon Organized Crime series – has been translated into several languages.

Soraya has a Bachelor of Arts Degree in Arts & Culture from Erasmus University Rotterdam.

Apart from writing and indulging in chocolate pastries much too often, Soraya Naomi is also an avid reader. She has a passionate obsession with the written word and reads many genres but favors intense stories where the male character loves fiercely, without remorse or boundaries. She adores Historical Romances, New Adult, Dark Romances, Romantic Suspense, and PNR. And she welcomes all recommendations!

Her debut novel *For Fallon (Chicago Syndicate, #1)* was released on July 26, 2014. She's honored that *For Fallon* won "Best Breakout Novel 2014" in the Novel Grounds Semi Annual Literary Awards.

For more information about the novel and author:
WEBSITE - sorayanaomi.com
FACEBOOK - facebook.com/sorayanaomi.author

READER GROUP - facebook.com/groups/chicagosyndicate

INSTAGRAM - instagram.com/soraya_naomi

TIKTOK - tiktok.com/@sorayanaomi_author

SUBSCRIBE TO NEWSLETTER - https://www.subscribepage.com/newslettersorayanaomi